The Sleepless
Little Vampire

The Sleepless Little Vampire

RICHARD EGIELSKI

ARTHUR A. LEVINE BOOKS
An Imprint of Scholastic Inc.

Library of Congress Cataloging-in-Publication Data

Egielski, Richard.
The sleepless little vampire / Richard Egielski. — 1st ed.   p. cm.
Summary: A young vampire, unable to sleep, tries to figure out whether it is the howling of a werewolf,
the clacking of skeletons, or something else that is keeping him awake.
ISBN 978-0-545-14597-8 (hardcover : alk. paper) [1. Bedtime — Fiction. 2. Vampires — Fiction.] I. Title.
PZ7.E3215Skm 2011   [E] — dc22   2010032096

10 9 8 7 6 5 4 3 2 1   11 12 13 14 15

Book design by Elizabeth B. Parisi

First edition, June 2011
Printed in Singapore   46

The art for this book was created using ink and watercolors.

To Sleepless Denise and D. Awdrey-Gore

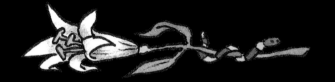

Why can't I sleep?
What could it be?

Is it—

the spider spitting?
THOOP!—THOOP!

Maybe it's—

the bats flitting?

FLAPPITY! — FLAP!

Or something else —

the cockroaches crawling?
SCRATCHITY-SCRATCH!

Could it be —

the werewolf bawling?
AWHOO!—AWHOO!

That's loud, but so are—

the skeletons clacking! CLICKITY-CLACK!

And —

the blue witch cackling! HEH—HEH-HEH!

All around me—

the ghosts are booing.

BOO! — BOO! And can it be? —

my room's soft-shoeing!?

No! That's not it. Don't you see?

It wasn't *bedtime* yet for me.

GOOD MORNING, NIGHT CREATURES!

Now, I don't want to hear a peep!

Everybody go —

to sleep.

Zzzz...